Changes, Changes

Changes, Changes

By PAT HUTCHINS

Aladdin Paperbacks

[STORIES]
E

III

Aladdin Paperbacks
An imprint of Simon & Schuster
Children's Publishing Division
1230 Avenue of the Americas
New York, NY 10020
First Aladdin Paperbacks edition, 1987
First paperbacks edition, 1973
Also available in a hardcover edition from Simon & Schuster Books for Young Readers

Manufactured in China

40 39 38 37 36 35 34 33

Library of Congress Cataloging-in-Publication Data

Hutchins, Pat, date.
    Changes, changes.

    Summary: Two wooden dolls rearrange wooden building
blocks to form various objects.
    [1. Toys—Fiction.   2. Stories without words]
I. Title.
[PZ7.H96165Ch   1987]   [E]   86-22331
ISBN 978-0-689-71137-4
0711 SCP

For Elsie and Bob Bruce